This book belongs to:

_____

**Ladybird**

Published by Ladybird Books Ltd
27 Wrights Lane London W8 5TZ
A Penguin Company
5 7 9 10 8 6 4

© LADYBIRD BOOKS LTD MCMXCVIII

Printed in Italy

# Operation
# Badger

written by Elizabeth Dale
illustrated by David Kearney

One night, Jenny was just going to bed, when her dad called from his study.

"Jenny! Matthew! Caroline!" he cried. "Come and see!"

Jenny turned and ran back down the stairs. She loved having a dad who was a vet. He was always showing her animals that were brought to him for treatment.

Matthew and Caroline, Jenny's brother and sister, rushed in, too. In a cage in the middle of the surgery lay a large, grey shape.

"A badger!" said Jenny.
"Oh, it's beautiful."

"She's been attacked by a dog," said Jenny's dad.

"Ahh! Poor thing!" said Caroline.

"She's all right now," said Mr Walsh. "Fortunately someone found her and brought her here, otherwise she could have died. But I've treated her wounds and now she just needs good nursing care."

"I'll help!" cried Jenny. "I'll stay up all night and nurse her!"

Mr Walsh smiled. When any animal needed special care, Jenny was always there offering to help look after it.

"I don't think you need to stay up all night," smiled Mr Walsh, "but I'm sure you can help tomorrow."

The next morning, the badger was looking much brighter. She was wearing a huge collar round her neck.

"What's that?" Jenny asked her dad.

"An Elizabethan collar," he said. "It's named after the first Queen Elizabeth, who used to wear collars a bit like this. It stops the badger chewing the wound on her leg."

"We'll call her Elizabeth, then,"
said Jenny, who liked to name
all the animals. "Betty for short.
Hello, Betty!"

Betty came over to the wire mesh
of her cage.

"Don't go poking your fingers in!"
warned Mr Walsh. "Badgers bite,
and boy, do I know it!"

Jenny brought her best friend Tom to see Betty after school. Betty was fast asleep when they looked into her cage.

"She's beautiful!" whispered Tom.

"Can we watch you feed her when she wakes up?" Jenny asked her dad.

"All right," said Mr Walsh.

Mr Walsh opened a tin of dog food for Betty's supper.

"Dog food!" said Tom, pulling a face. "Can't we give her bread and milk instead?"

"No," smiled Mr Walsh. "She eats meat in the wild and she needs it here, too. But I'll give her some biscuits as well."

Betty tucked into her supper greedily while all the children watched.

"Can we keep her, Daddy?" asked Caroline.

Mr Walsh shook his head.

"She needs to go back to the wild, but not until she's better."

"I hope she's not better for a long time, then!" said Caroline.

"Caroline!" cried Jenny, but she knew just what Caroline meant.

Jenny went to see Betty every morning as soon as she got up and when she got back from school. If Betty was awake, she would come snuffling over to the wire mesh as soon as Jenny walked in.

"She likes you," said her dad. "Probably because you spend so much time with her!"

Jenny smiled. She loved watching Betty. She was so adorable.

"Her wounds are getting better now, aren't they?" she said.

"Yes," said her dad. "I think we should release her tomorrow night."

"Can I come and watch?" asked Jenny.

"Of course," said Mr Walsh.

The whole family went to say goodbye to Betty. She'd been found in the woods behind their house. Mr Walsh knew there was a badger sett there, so that was where she was set free.

It was already dark as Betty stepped out of her cage. She sniffed at the ground and the air, and then, without a backward glance, ran off into the woods.

"She didn't even say goodbye," said Caroline, sadly.

"She's well and she's free," said Jenny, wiping a tear from her eye. "That's all that matters!"

The next day Jenny missed Betty terribly. She missed rushing down to her in the morning, and at school she couldn't concentrate on her lessons.

That night, she sat in the lounge and gazed out into the darkness.

"Goodnight, Betty!" she called softly.

"You daft thing!" said Matthew, creeping in. "She can't hear you! She'll have forgotten all about you!"

Jenny picked up a cushion to throw at her brother, but a sudden movement in the garden caught her eye.

It was Betty! Jenny couldn't believe her eyes.

"Dad!" she cried. "Come and look! Betty's come back!"

"Well, well!" said Mr Walsh, rushing in. "She's come to say goodbye after all!"

"Not goodbye," said Jenny, sliding open the patio door, "but hello! Hello, Betty!"

Jenny threw some dog biscuits over to Betty and she ate them greedily. When she'd finished, she snuffled around the garden while the whole family gathered around. And then she turned and ran away again.

Tom was thrilled when Jenny told him what had happened. The next evening he came round to the Walsh's house and waited with Jenny for Betty to come. And sure enough, she did.

"Dear me, I'm going to have to keep on buying extra dog biscuits!" said Mrs Walsh, pretending to be cross.

21

Betty came every night for weeks. She was like an extra dinner guest, uninvited but always welcome. But one night Betty didn't appear. She didn't come the next night either, even though Jenny waited until long past bedtime.

"Don't be sad!" said her dad, tucking her into bed. "This means that Betty doesn't need us any more. She's a proper wild badger again."

"No!" cried Jenny. "I'm sure something's wrong. Betty wouldn't just disappear like that. Something must have happened to her!"

When Betty didn't come again the next night, Jenny was very worried.

"All right, Jenny!" said her dad, putting on his coat. "The only way we're going to put your mind at rest is by finding her. Come on, let's go to her sett."

Jenny grabbed her coat and followed her dad. The wood was strangely eerie at night. Twigs cracked loudly under her feet and once an owl swooped low overhead, giving Jenny a fright.

"Shh!" said her dad as they approached the sett.

Jenny tiptoed quietly forward.

"Oh, dear!" said Mr Walsh quietly.

"What is it?" asked Jenny fearfully.

Her dad shone the torch at a pile of freshly dug earth.

"It looks as though someone's destroyed the sett!" he said.

Jenny burst into tears.

"How can people do that kind of thing?" she wailed. "And what about Betty! Have they killed Betty?"

"I expect she's all right," said Mr Walsh, putting his arm around Jenny. "This sett is probably joined to others and she'll be safe somewhere in there."

But Jenny wasn't so sure. Why else hadn't Betty been to visit her?

Jenny's mum bought her a toy badger to remind her of Betty. Jenny cuddled it every night. She couldn't stop wondering what had happened to Betty.

She still looked for Betty every night. Tom often came and sat with her, staring out into the garden, just in case.

One night, Jenny had turned to go, when Tom caught hold of her arm.

"Look!" he whispered. "Just look!"

Jenny turned and stared in amazement. Trotting towards the window was not one badger, but four! Betty was in front and behind her came three adorable badger cubs!

"That's why she didn't come before!" said Mr Walsh. "She's been too busy with her babies. What do you think of that, Jenny?"

But Jenny was too happy to speak. Betty hadn't been killed, and she hadn't forgotten all about Jenny. And now, instead of one badger coming to visit her each night, she'd got four!

31

**Mr Walsh tells you more about…
catching injured wild animals**

Whilst an injured bird usually cannot
fly, many other wounded animals can
still move very fast. Even a deer with
two broken legs can run quite
quickly. This makes catching them
very difficult. Only a hedgehog will
just curl up into a ball when afraid,
making it easy to catch.

I never chase after an injured animal or bird. This would only frighten it and make things worse. I try to block off all escape routes, keeping myself between the animal and any danger, such as a road. Then I move towards the animal slowly, keeping low, and catch it with a net or grasper. I let larger animals run into the nets that I have set up.

# Meet the characters…

**Mr Walsh**
*a vet*

**Mrs Walsh**
*a veterinary nurse*

**Jenny Walsh**
*nine years old*

## Matthew Walsh
*eleven years old*

## Caroline Walsh
*four years old*

## Tom Henderson
*nine years old and Jenny's best friend*

## Jepp
*the family collie dog*

To catch Betty, I used a grasper. This is a hollow pole with a loop of rope that I slipped over her neck to hold her tight. Some animals, such as foxes and deer are far too quick for a grasper, so I set up large nets around them.